KLOOZ

After School
Ghost Hunter

by J. Banscherus
translated by Daniel C. Baron
illustrated by Ralf Butschkow

Librarian Reviewer
Marci Peschke
Librarian, Dallas Independent School District
MA Education Reading Specialist, Stephen F. Austin State University
Learning Resources Endorsement, Texas Women's University

Reading Consultant
Mary Evenson
Middle School Teacher, Edina Public Schools, MN
MA in Education, University of Minnesota

STONE ARCH BOOKS
Minneapolis   San Diego

First published in the United States in 2007
by Stone Arch Books,
151 Good Counsel Drive, P.O. Box 669,
Mankato, Minnesota 56002
www.stonearchbooks.com

First published by Arena Books,
Rottendorfer str. 16, D-97074,
Würzburg, Germany

Library of Congress Cataloging-in-Publication Data
Banscherus, Jürgen.
  [Rosarote Schulgespenst. English]
  After School Ghost Hunter / by J. Banscherus; translated by Daniel
C. Baron; illustrated by Ralf Butschkow.
  p. cm. — (Pathway Books – Klooz)
  Summary: When the school custodian claims the hallways are
haunted, Klooz decides to find out what is really happening.
  ISBN-13: 978-1-59889-342-7 (hardcover)
  ISBN-10: 1-59889-342-4 (hardcover)
  ISBN-13: 978-1-59889-441-7 (paperback)
  ISBN-10: 1-59889-441-2 (paperback)
  [1. Ghosts—Fiction. 2. Schools—Fiction. 3. Mystery and detective
stories.] I. Baron, Daniel C. II. Butschkow, Ralf, ill. III. Title.

PZ7.B22927Af 2007
[Fic]—dc22   2006027195

Art Director: Heather Kindseth
Graphic Designer: Kay Fraser

1 2 3 4 5 6 12 11 10 09 08 07

Printed in the United States of America

TOP SECRET

Table of contents

KLOOZ
After School
Ghost Hunter

CHAPTER 1

Ghost Hunter

Most great detectives were never very good students. I am not as famous as Sherlock Holmes, but I am a bad student. A private detective like me needs exciting adventures, dangerous chases, and dark secrets, otherwise I get bored to death. And what does school have to offer? Spelling, multiplication and division, the life cycle of the frog, healthy eating, and other boring subjects.

That's why I sometimes fall asleep in class and only wake up when it's time for recess.

Why don't we discuss blackmail letters in English class? Why don't we figure out how much a day in jail or sending a SWAT team to a bank robbery costs in math class? I certainly wouldn't fall asleep in classes like that, and neither would most of my classmates.

With your English skills you are probably going to be a purse snatcher's blackmailer or a math teacher.

CRIME
ROBBERY
BURGLARS
SWINDLERS
THIEVES

My mom says that I look at the whole world like one big crime case.

She thinks it's good that my time at school isn't all about robbery, theft, and fraud.

Most people don't want to become private detectives. They want to become nurses, bus drivers, or computer workers.

All these people have to learn normal things in school.

It's funny how adults always seem to know what's normal.

All anyone has to do is turn on the TV and learn how the world is really not normal at all.

But why am I talking about school? Simple, because my latest case was there.

Everyone knows that I love chewing gum. My favorite brand is Carpenter's Chewing Gum. You can only get it at my friend Olga's newspaper stand. For all the money I have spent on chewing gum this last year I could have bought a mountain bike with twenty-seven gears and super shocks.

The last time I was at the newspaper stand, I ran into Boss. The name of our school custodian is Mr. Boston. Everybody, except for the principal, just calls him "Boss."

He is the nicest custodian in the whole world. Heck, he is the nicest in the whole universe. No matter what kind of mess the students make, he never loses his cool.

"I was a kid once too, you know," he always says, and laughs.

A couple of weeks ago he wasn't like that. I was at Olga's, standing behind Boss's enormous back.

I couldn't see his face, but I could tell he was nervous.

Olga seemed to notice it too. She asked, "Is there something wrong at school?"

Boss bent over and whispered so quietly that I could hardly hear what he was saying.

"It's haunted!" he said.

"What's haunted?" asked Olga.

"The school."

Olga was surprised. "Since when?"

"For two days now," Boss answered. "The haunting always happens between ten p.m. and midnight."

Olga stuck a piece of candy in her mouth.

Since she gave up smoking, she goes through a lot of candy. Mom thinks it would be better if more people would do that. Stop smoking, I mean.

"How do you know it's haunted?" was Olga's next question. Man, she was asking questions like a real detective, just the way I do it.

"I see shadows, unearthly shadows!" Boss said.

"And do you hear noises, too?" asked Olga.

Boss shook his head.

"Why don't you just find out what's making the shadows?" said Olga.

"I don't have a death wish!" the custodian cried. "What would happen if it really was a ghost? Then what?"

Olga interrupted him. "There is no such thing as ghosts," she said firmly. "And there is really no such thing as school ghosts."

At that point Olga noticed I was standing there.

"Hello, my angel!" she greeted me.

I've told her a thousand times not to call me that when other people were around. It's embarrassing.

"How many packs do you need today?" she asked.

My allowance was almost all gone. I only had enough for one pack.

Olga laid the pack on the counter and made my last dollar disappear. Then she turned to Boss. "You should hire Klooz. He's the best."

"The best what?" the school custodian asked.

Olga moved the candy from one corner of her mouth to the other.

"The best private detective," she said. "If anyone can find out who is haunting your school, it's Klooz."

Boss stared at me. Of course he knew that I worked as a private detective. Everybody knew that in our neighborhood. But he probably believed, as most grown-ups did, that I only tracked down missing dogs, stolen jackets, and swiped chewing gum.

Boss adjusted his glasses and asked, "Have you ever hunted ghosts?"

"Of course," I told him.

"And what did you find out about them?" he said.

I remembered my case of the blue merry-go-round. During the case, I met evil spirits disguised as guinea pigs. Okay, they were just guinea pigs. But doesn't that count? I mean, I thought they were ghosts.

"There are no ghosts," I answered. "Real ghosts don't exist."

Boss looked thoughtful. It is funny that such a big guy was afraid of a few shadows.

"Okay then," he said. "What will it cost me if you take the case?"

"Five packs of gum," I replied.

"And if you can't find out who is haunting my school?"

"Oh, I'll solve the case," I promised him.

Boss stuck out his hand for me to shake. "All right then," he said. "You'll get your five packs. What's next?"

"Will you be home this evening?" I asked.

He nodded.

"I'll be there at nine thirty," I said.

CHAPTER 2

The Dark School

This case would be easy. Of course there were no such things as ghosts. What could possibly go wrong?

Before I got the case of the school ghost, my mom was working during the day at the hospital. Because I had so many cases during that time, my grades were really bad. That bothered my mom. So she changed her work schedule at the hospital so that she could be around to make sure I was doing my homework.

That night, my mom was going out with some friends.

At nine fifteen she came into my room. I was on my bed listening to some music on the radio and reading about famous crimes in a book that I had checked out from the library.

My mom gave me a kiss. "See you tomorrow," she said. "Sleep well."

"See you tomorrow, Mom."

"Will you make breakfast for both of us?" she asked.

"Yup."

"Cereal and coffee with cream?"

"Sure, Mom."

Before she left, she looked deep into my eyes.

She always does that when she thinks I am hiding something important from her.

"Do you have a new case, Klooz?" she asked.

I nodded. "It has to do with ghosts."

She laughed. "Well, at least it has nothing to do with crime."

In my closet I had already put together everything that a detective needs for nightly ghost hunts: a flashlight, a warm sweater, a key chain with homemade skeleton keys, and a bottle for milk.

The pack of Carpenter's that I had bought at Olga's would come along too, of course. Without my gum I wouldn't even try to find a missing sock. That gum inspired me!

I packed everything in the seventeen pockets of my new vest and started off.

This was a funny case.

Boss was over six feet tall and as wide as a refrigerator. He could carry a piano through the school as if it was light as a feather, yet he was afraid of ghosts.

Boss lives next door to the school. It was exactly nine thirty when I rang Boss's doorbell. He came to the door right away. "Come in, Klooz," he said in a friendly tone.

I shook my head. "You have to lock me in."

His face turned into a huge question mark. "Lock you in?" he stuttered. "Where?"

Sometimes adults don't understand detectives. "Where else?" I asked. "In the school! I've got to find out who the ghosts are, right? You can let me out again after midnight."

"I see," he said as he took a keychain from a hook next to the door. "But isn't that too dangerous?"

"There is no such thing as ghosts,"
I said.

Boss hesitated. "If something happens
to you, it's my fault," he said. "Then I'd
lose my job."

I put my hand on his arm.

"What could possibly happen?" I asked. "The whole thing is probably just someone's idea of a joke."

Boss and I strolled over to the school, and he unlocked one of the doors. Before he locked me in, he said, "If you need me, just scream. Scream as loud as you can and I'll come and help you. I promise."

I grinned but said nothing. A guy who is that afraid of ghosts was going to help me?

At night everything looks different. Parks look like deep forests, houses change into scary dungeons.

Up until now I had always thought I could find my way around the school with my eyes shut.

But in the dim light cast by the streetlights outside, I felt like I was on a different planet.

I crashed into walls, tripped over steps, and fell over a backpack that someone had left in the middle of the hallway.

I was not afraid. Not really. I knew there was no such thing as ghosts.

But standing in a corner near the teachers' lounge, it wouldn't have surprised me if I saw a bunch of ghosts, vampires, and werewolves.

So I turned on my flashlight. I immediately felt better. It could be that by turning on the flashlight I had chased away the ghosts or whatever was haunting the building, but in that moment I didn't care. The main thing was that my fear disappeared. I felt brave enough to come out of the corner.

On my trip through the three-story school, I found four empty soda bottles in the teachers' lounge and a mouse in classroom 2A.

I found something else, too.

The door to the underground bicycle storage was open! Anyone could easily enter the school this way. Not only that, but anyone could come in this way without being seen.

Hours later, when Boss let me out of the school after midnight, I told him about the open door.

He just shrugged his shoulders.

"Did you find anything else?" he asked.

I shook my head.

"I saw you go through the whole school with your flashlight," Boss said. "You probably chased them away."

"Probably," I said.

"But I can't leave the school lights on every night," said Boss. "That would cost a fortune!"

While we were talking, a cloud passed over the moon and the school yard grew very dark.

"I'll take you home," Boss said.

"You'll lock me in the school again tomorrow night, right?" I asked.

"I don't know," he mumbled. "I really don't like this."

"I don't either," I answered.

On the way home thoughts went through my head like a rollercoaster.

Did Boss simply forget to lock the door to the underground bicycle storage room?

Or was there something else going on? Was someone trying to throw me off track?

Before I went to sleep, I decided that next time I would leave my flashlight in my backpack. I would do my hunt in the dark.

Even if the school was crawling with headless ghosts and monsters.

CHAPTER 3

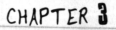

The Glowing Ghost

The next morning, after only five hours of sleep, I was tired. I only realized it during second hour, when Mr. Krank returned our English tests.

I got a C minus. My last grade was a D, so I guess that mom making sure I did my homework was paying off! Our teacher didn't quite see it that way.

"I want to meet with your mom," he said with a serious look.

Actually he always looks that way, even if you get an A.

"Why?" I asked.

"You could be a great student," he said, "but you get one C after another."

I started to explain to him that most famous detectives were bad students. But Mr. Krank wouldn't let me continue.

"Tell your mom she should call me,"
he growled. "During recess if possible."

On my way home I stopped by Olga's.
She was in her newsstand eating soup that
smelled like garlic.

"Would you like some?" she asked.

I shook my head. I would only eat soup
with garlic if I was starving to death.

"Would you like a soda?" she asked.

She placed a glass on the counter for
me and put her soup bowl in a little sink
in the corner of her newspaper stand.

"So, tell me what's going on," she said.

"I got a C minus in English,"
I complained.

She punched me in the ribs so hard
that I had to gasp for air.

"That's terrible," she said, "but I'm not talking about that. What's happening with the school ghost?"

I then reported everything that happened the night before. Olga can listen like nobody else in the whole world. That's one of the reasons I like talking with her.

"Something isn't right," she said when I was finished.

I thought the same thing.

"I have the feeling Boss has a secret," she said.

"You said it," I agreed. "But what kind of secret?"

"I have no idea, Klooz," she answered. "You should keep an eye on him."

At home it wasn't as bad as I thought it would be. When my mom saw the C minus on my test, she just sighed. When I told her she needed to call Mr. Krank, she got quiet.

Funny. It usually seemed like nothing was more important than my grades to her.

"Is something wrong?" I asked her.

She hugged me.

"A little girl died last night at the hospital," she said quietly. "It was awful. In comparison to that, a C minus is nothing to get too upset about."

"Was the little girl very sick?" I wanted to know.

"Very," she said.

That afternoon I was quiet around the apartment. I played my music softly and even finished my homework.

Mom was really happy when I showed it to her. I was happy too, because she smiled again.

That night, I went over to Boss's house again. Like the night before, he didn't really want to lock me in the school. Either he was afraid of losing his job or there was something else going on.

Once I was inside the school, I found a place on the ground floor near a window. I could watch the playground, the school gate, and Boss's house. If anything unusual happened, I was sure to see it.

When it was completely dark, I heard noises coming from the floor above me. As I looked out the window, I could see that everything was normal at Boss's house. If I wasn't mistaken, he was sitting with his wife in the living room in front of the TV.

It was time for action!

I grabbed my backpack and crept up the stairs. I reached the teacher's lounge without a single squeak to give me away.

The noises were definitely coming from there. The whispering, knocking, and walking back and forth really did sound like ghost noises.

I could see a dull light shining through underneath the door.

Someone was probably working in the room by flashlight. What should I do? Should I wait until they come out? Should I go to Boss's house and call the police from there?

I had to admit, I wasn't sure that there weren't ghosts in the room. Even though I had watched everything from my hiding place, I hadn't seen anyone enter the room.

Could ghosts go through walls? All of
the windows that I had checked on my way
through the school were closed and locked.

There was only one other way to get into the school: the bicycle storage room.

I went downstairs to check. Sure enough, just like the night before, the door was open. This had to be how the ghosts got in. I reached into my backpack and got out my last piece of gum. I calmed down and began to think about this mystery

Ghosts didn't enter buildings through bicycle storage rooms. They didn't need to do that. That meant that whoever was in the teacher's lounge was a normal human being. I simply had to wait here until they wanted to go home. Then I could follow them and find out who they were.

Then I heard a sound behind me. I turned and for the first time in my life swallowed a piece of gum.

On the stairs there was a ghost, a real live ghost! My hand reached into my backpack, grabbed the flashlight, and turned it on.

A glowing ghost was standing in front of me. Under his robe you could see bright yellow running shoes. My first thought was that ghosts don't wear shoes.

The figure turned and ran up the stairs. I have no idea what I was thinking, but I ran after him. You can't really be afraid of a ghost wearing yellow sneakers, right?

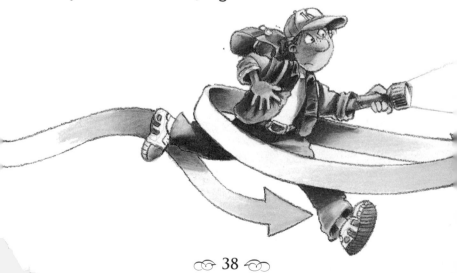

As I chased the ghost, I had only
one question. What in the world was
underneath that sheet? If it was a skeleton
with his skull underneath his arm, it
would be moving differently.

This ghost was definitely a person.

Soon I was only three feet away from
the figure. This was my chance. I jumped
at the ghost and grabbed at the sheet.

CHAPTER 4

My Black Eye

The figure waved his arms around wildly and then fell hard on the floor. My flashlight also fell to the floor. I heard breaking glass and then everything went dark.

Anyone who knows me knows I hate violence. I always try to solve every problem peacefully. But in the darkness that didn't count anymore. Maybe neither one of us wanted to fight. Maybe we both just wanted to get away from the other. But the sheet was all over the place.

We were both so wrapped up in it that we started to fight each other.

I took a punch to the eye and a blow to the stomach that knocked the wind out of me.

Suddenly the door to the teacher's lounge opened and three or four figures ran out of the room. The ghost freed himself from my grip and started running too.

I guessed where they were heading: the bicycle storage room. Even though I should have pursued them, I decided not to. After the wild fight I didn't think it was worth it.

Now at least I had a clue. During the fight I tore off a piece of the ghost's sheet. This cloth could lead me to the ghost itself.

Carefully I stood up and looked into the teachers' lounge. In the dull light from the street lamp there wasn't much to see.

On a big table in the middle of the room there were books and notebooks. Sports equipment was stored under the windowsills.

In the sink there were empty cups and a few glasses. It didn't look like anything in here was worth stealing. What did the strange figures want?

I left the school building through the bicycle storage room and walked over to Boss's house.

He was still sitting in front of the TV with his wife.

"What happened?" he cried as he pointed to my black eye.

I could feel it starting to swell.

"I got hit by the ghost," I said, and explained in a few short sentences what had happened.

"So it isn't a ghost," he said.

"No ghost."

"Real people," he said.

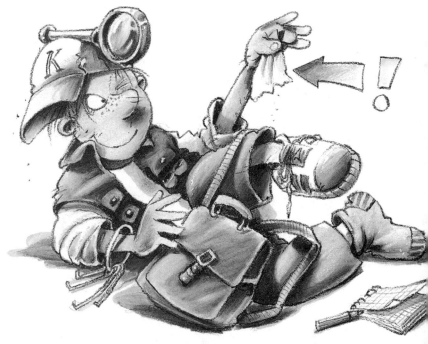

"With yellow shoes," I added.

"And now what?" he asked.

"I have a plan," I told him before making my way home.

* * *

That night I slept like a rock. I didn't hear the alarm clock. I didn't even wake up when Mom opened my window. I awoke when she screamed.

"What happened to your eye?" she cried.

I was so tired, I had no idea what she was talking about.

"I'm taking you to the doctor," she said as she pulled the blanket off of me.

"It's no big deal, Mom," I said. "I hit it on something."

Somehow I was able to convince her we didn't need to go to the doctor.

I really didn't have time. I was going to solve the case that very day. I knew I would. I could feel that from head to toe. But in order to do that, I had to go to school as fast as possible.

My eye was swollen almost shut.

I could only see through a very small slit. But that didn't matter now. As long as my other eye still worked, I didn't care.

Of course, everybody at school made jokes about it. I didn't care about that, either, because I made a discovery during first hour. It was so amazing that it nearly took my breath away.

Mr. Krank, our teacher, was limping. He also had a deep scratch on his left cheek that didn't look like he had cut himself shaving. Was that scratch from me? Was Mr. Krank the school ghost? How was that possible?

During recess and lunch I watched our teacher very carefully. No one except Mr. Krank was limping. No one else had a broken nose or black eye or any other injury. Mr. Krank was my only suspect.

After school I followed him.

He doesn't live far from school, and he walked, as usual. I followed about a hundred and fifty feet behind him so he wouldn't see me. Mr. Krank didn't turn around a single time.

When he got home, he grabbed the mail from his mailbox, and hurried inside. I waited a few minutes and then got closer for a better look.

There was nothing strange in front of his house. But in the backyard I saw clothes drying on a clothesline. Very interesting.

I pushed my way through tall bushes and then hid behind a pine tree. There were pants, shirts, and bedsheets flapping in the wind.

And one of the bedsheets was torn!

I ran over to look at the sheet more closely. What I found didn't surprise me in the least. A small piece of the sheet was missing. Aha!

In my wildest dreams I never thought I would catch Mr. Krank being a ghost. At that moment I heard a man's angry voice behind me.

CHAPTER 5

Surprise Party

Mr. Krank was standing right behind me. His glasses were sitting crooked on his nose and his hair was all messed up.

"Just what do you think you're doing, young man?" he snapped.

I took a deep breath. After all, Mr. Krank was my teacher. He was the one who gave me all of my grades.

"You're haunting the school," I said.

He looked at me as if I had turned into a cow with two heads.

"I-I-I beg your pardon?" he stuttered.

"You're haunting the school," I said with a louder voice. I pointed to his bright yellow shoes. "You had those shoes on last night."

I took out the piece of sheet that I had torn off the night before and held it next to the sheet on the wash line. It was a perfect match.

"And you were wearing this sheet," I said.

It seemed as if Mr. Krank had shrunk several inches. He took off his glasses and rubbed his head. Finally he said, "Come into the house, Klooz. I think I have some things to tell you."

That's how I learned a story so unbelievable that it had to be true.

It all started when the teachers decided to do something special for Mr. Boston's fiftieth birthday.

The classrooms and hallways were supposed to be decorated and a statue of our custodian was to be placed in a corner of the schoolyard.

Of course no one wanted to make ribbons, pictures, flags, and a life-size plaster statue at home alone.

At that point I interrupted Mr. Krank.

"So you decided to make all the decorations together in the school," I said.

My teacher nodded.

"And you pretended to be a ghost in order to keep Mr. Boston away," I said.

Mr. Krank nodded again. "Sometimes we had to carry the statue and decorations from one part of the building to another. So I put on the sheet and walked in front of my friends. Until yesterday it worked great," he told me.

"Mr. Boston was afraid to enter the building on Wednesday and Thursday nights. Who would have guessed that he'd ask a private detective for help?"

Mr. Krank touched his cheek. "You have quite the punch," he said.

I pointed to my eye. "You too, Mr. Krank."

For a while we were both quiet.

"Are you going to tell on us?" he asked

I didn't have to think very long about that.

"Of course not," I replied. "When is Mr. Boston's birthday?"

"Tomorrow," Mr. Krank answered.

"And are you finished with the decorations?" I wanted to know.

"Yes, we are going to put everything up tonight."

He pointed outside where the clothes were flapping in the wind. "I'll have to play ghost just one more time."

"Okay. You don't need to worry about me interfering," I said.

When he brought me to his door, Mr. Krank slipped five dollars into my hand.

"Thanks for keeping quiet," he said. "Buy yourself something with this."

More gum, I thought.

* * *

The birthday was a huge success. Boss was completely surprised. And he loved the life-size statue.

After our principal gave a wonderful speech, the teachers sang a song they had written about Mr. Boston.

Then Boss took me aside. "There was a ghost again last night," he whispered. "This time it was real, believe me. It was white as a sheet and had little black eyes. It was terrible!"

"That was the last time," I said.

"How can you be so sure?" he asked.

"I just am," I said. Boss reached into his pocket and took out five packs of gum.

"Here's your fee," he said. "But I get back every cent if the ghost returns."

"It's a deal," I said.

That afternoon I dropped by Olga's newspaper stand. I wasn't the only customer.

Mr. Krank was ahead of me in line. He was buying a pack of Carpenter's gum. "Just wanted to try it," he said and winked.

"A nice man," Olga said after Mr. Krank disappeared.

"Nice? I don't know about that."

"What do you have against him?"
she asked.

"Well he is my teacher, you know," I
answered. "Besides that he gave me this
black eye the other night."

"What!" Olga was shocked.

Then I told her all about how I solved
the case of the after-school ghost. As I
talked, Olga kept laughing out loud.

"So he is a nice man," she said when I was finished. "A teacher who dresses up as a ghost can't be all bad."

What could I say? When Olga is right, she's right.

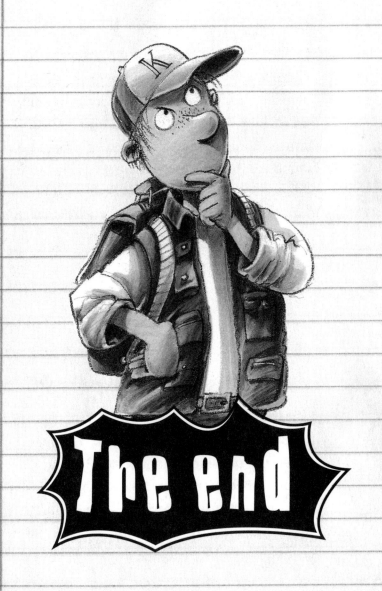

About the Author

Jürgen Banscherus is a worldwide phenomenon. There are almost a million Klooz books in print, and they have been translated into Spanish, Danish, Thai, Chinese, and eleven other languages. He has worked as a newspaper writer, a research scientist, and a teacher. His first book for children was published in 1985. He lives with his family in Germany.

About the Illustrator

Ralf Butschkow was born in Berlin. He works as a freelance graphic designer and illustrator, and has published more than 50 books for children. Critics have praised his work as "thoroughly enjoyable," "creatively original," and "highly recommended."

Glossary

blackmail (BLAK-mayl)—threatening to tell someone's secrets unless they pay you; blackmail is against the law

inspired (in-SPYRD)—full of ideas and energy

limp (LIMP)—walking with difficulty, usually because you are hurt or in pain

plaster (PLASS-tur)—a type of paste that turns hard. Plaster is used to cover walls and ceilings, and sometimes to make statues

slit (SLIT)—a small or narrow opening

SWAT team (SWOT teem)—a special group of law enforcers. SWAT stands for **S**pecial **W**eapons **a**nd **T**actics. Tactics are plans.

Discussion Questions

1. Mr. Boston thought his school was haunted. Do you think there are such things as ghosts? Why or why not?

2. What convinced Klooz that Mr. Krank was the fake ghost? What were the clues that he found that proved it was the teacher?

3. At the end of the story, Mr. Krank goes to Olga's newsstand and buys some of Klooz's favorite chewing gum for himself. Why do you think he wants to try it?

Writing Prompts

1. The teachers at Klooz's school must really like Mr. Boston to give him such a great surprise party. Imagine that your family and friends give you a surpise party. What kind of food will you have? What kind of presents do you get? Describe the scene.

2. Klooz doesn't believe in ghosts, but when he's alone in the dark school, he starts to imagine things. Have you ever thought you saw things in the dark or late at night? And then, when you turned on the lights, it turned out to be something else? Write a story and tell what happened.

More Klooz for

by J. Banscherus

Clues in the Car Wash

*Olga has a case for her favorite detective, Klooz.
Someone scratched her new luxury car. Soon Klooz
hears that lots of cars in town are getting scratched
and scraped. The trail of clues leads him to the car
wash on Main Street, where Klooz discovers that
cleaning cars can be a dirty business!*

Mystery Fans!

KLOOZ

Trouble Under the Big Top

by J. Banscherus

STONE ARCH Mystery

Trouble Under the Big Top

The Zampano Circus is in town! Vanessa is the best juggler in the circus, but she keeps making the same mistake during each show: one of her juggling pins flies into the audience! And then it flies back! Can Klooz solve the strange puzzle of the boomerang juggler?

Internet Sites

Do you want to know more about subjects related to this book? Or are you interested in learning about other topics? Then check out FactHound, a fun, easy way to find Internet sites.

Our investigative staff has already sniffed out great sites for you!

Here's how to use FactHound:

1. Visit *www.facthound.com*

2. Select your grade level.

3. To learn more about subjects related to this book, type in the book's ISBN number: **1598893424**.

4. Click the **Fetch It** button.

FactHound will fetch the best Internet sites for you!